DIVINE MELODY: THE ESSENCE OF RAAM NAAM

AMAR PRAKASH TRIPATHI

Contents

Foreword

In the vast tapestry of human existence, there exists a universal language that transcends boundaries, religions, and cultures—the language of divine melody. It is a language woven into the very fabric of our souls, resonating with the eternal vibrations that connect us to the divine.

In the pages that follow, you are about to embark on a profound journey through the mystical realms of spirituality and self-discovery. "Divine Melody: The Essence of Raam Naam" is not merely a book; it is an invitation to explore the profound depths of the human spirit through the transformative power of sacred vibrations.

Raam Naam, the divine name of Lord Rama, is not just a sequence of syllables; it is a cosmic vibration that has echoed through the corridors of time, guiding seekers on their quest for truth and enlightenment. This book delves into the essence of Raam Naam, unlocking its secrets and unraveling the divine melody that lies within.

As you turn the pages, you will encounter stories, teachings, and insights that illuminate the path to spiritual awakening. The author has skillfully woven together ancient wisdom, personal reflections, and timeless truths to create a harmonious tapestry that resonates with the reader's heart and soul.

The journey of self-discovery is often accompanied by challenges, doubts, and uncertainties. Yet, within the sacred vibrations of Raam Naam, there is a source of strength, solace, and sublime joy. Through the pages of this book, you will discover the transformative power of chanting the divine name and the profound impact it can have on your inner landscape.

"Divine Melody" is an ode to the universal melody that pervades the cosmos—a melody that beckons us to rediscover our true nature and connect with the divine within. May this book serve as a guiding light on your spiritual journey, inspiring you to embrace the essence of Raam Naam and harmonize with the divine melody that echoes through eternity.

In the words of the ancient sages and mystics, let the divine melody guide you to the inner sanctum of your soul, where the essence of Raam Naam resides, waiting to be heard, felt, and lived.

Embark on this transformative journey, and may the divine melody lead you to the sublime heights of spiritual realization.

Jai Siya Raam,

Amar Prakash Tripathi

9th December 2023

Preface

In the symphony of existence, where the universe resonates with the harmonious vibrations of creation, there exists a celestial melody that transcends time and space – the Divine Melody of Raam Naam. This book, "Divine Melody: The Essence of Raam Naam," endeavors to explore the profound depths of this timeless and sacred sound, inviting readers on a spiritual journey that traverses the realms of the inner self and connects with the cosmic resonance of the divine.

Raam Naam, the sacred name of Lord Rama, is not merely a string of syllables; it is a vibrational key that unlocks the doors to spiritual awakening and inner transformation. Across cultures and epochs, mystics, saints, and seekers have attested to the transformative power of chanting the divine name. It is a practice that transcends religious boundaries and speaks to the universal longing for connection with the divine.

In the pages that follow, we delve into the essence of Raam Naam, exploring its significance in various spiritual traditions, its mystical resonance, and its potential to guide individuals on the path of self-realization. Drawing inspiration from ancient scriptures, wisdom traditions, and the experiences of those who have walked the path before us, "Divine Melody" serves as a guide for both beginners and seasoned seekers alike.

This book is not a theological treatise but a heartfelt exploration of the transformative power inherent in the repetition and contemplation of the divine name. It seeks to inspire readers to embark on their own personal journey of self-discovery and spiritual growth, using Raam Naam as a compass guiding them through the labyrinth of the human experience.

As you turn the pages, may you feel the resonance of the Divine Melody vibrating within your heart, echoing the eternal truth that unites all of creation. May this exploration into the essence of Raam Naam awaken within you a deeper understanding of your own divine nature and foster a sense of unity with the cosmic symphony that reverberates through the universe.

May the Divine Melody guide you on your spiritual journey, leading you to the inner sanctum of your soul, where the essence of Raam Naam unfolds as the timeless song of the divine.

Acknowledgements

I would like to express my heartfelt gratitude to everyone who played a pivotal role in the creation and completion of "Divine Melody: The Essence of Raam Naam." This journey has been an enriching and transformative experience, and I owe my deepest thanks to the following individuals:

My Father and Mother:

To my dear parents, whose love, encouragement, and unwavering belief in my abilities have been the foundation of my journey. Your sacrifices and boundless support have shaped not only this book but also my life. I am forever grateful for your love and inspiration.

Friends:

A heartfelt thank you to my friends who stood by me during the highs and lows of this creative process. Your encouragement, constructive feedback, and camaraderie have been a source of strength and motivation. Your friendship is treasured, and I am thankful for each of you.

Sanjeev jee:

A special acknowledgment goes to Sanjeev jee, whose unwavering support, wisdom, and guidance have been the guiding light throughout my life. Your mentorship, Guru-prasad has been invaluable, and I am profoundly grateful for your insights and encouragement. In addition to that, Your expertise and passion for the subject matter have added depth and authenticity to the pages of this book. I appreciate your dedication and the positive impact you have had/have thorough our interactions.

This book is a culmination of the collective efforts of those mentioned above and many more whose support has been instrumental. Each of you has played a significant role in bringing "Divine Melody: The Essence of Raam Naam" to life, and for that, I am truly grateful.

With heartfelt thanks,
Amar Prakash Tripathi

Prologue

In the tranquil embrace of eternity, where the celestial symphony of the cosmos resonates, there lies a sacred tale, a melodic journey that transcends the realms of mortal comprehension. This is the prologue to "Divine Melody: The Essence of Raam Naam."

In the heart of spiritual awakening, amidst the whispers of the divine breeze, we embark upon a pilgrimage of the soul. Our quest delves into the timeless essence of Raam Naam, a celestial melody that echoes through the corridors of existence. It is a hymn that transcends the barriers of language, a vibration that pulsates with the rhythm of cosmic harmony.

As we tread upon the sacred soil of this narrative, let us unveil the layers of understanding that cloak the profound wisdom within. Raam Naam, the sacred name that reverberates through the cosmos, is not merely a sequence of syllables but a portal to the ethereal realm. It is the key that unlocks the door to spiritual enlightenment, inviting us to dance in harmony with the cosmic dance of creation.

Within these pages, the seeker shall find echoes of ancient truths, whispered by sages and mystics who have walked the path of illumination. The narrative unfolds like petals of a celestial lotus, each revealing a fragment of the divine melody that orchestrates the cosmic dance of life.

Prepare, dear reader, to embark upon a journey of the soul—a journey where the mundane dissolves into the sublime, and the essence of Raam Naam becomes a beacon guiding us back to the source. Through the tapestry of simple words, woven with threads of profound meaning, we shall explore the infinite vistas of spirituality, seeking the divine melody that resonates within the recesses of our hearts.

May this odyssey awaken the dormant seeker within, and may the Divine Melody guide us on our quest for eternal truth and spiritual fulfillment.

ONE

THE CALL OF HARMONY

"Embark on a journey into the heart of spiritual resonance as we delve into the essence of Raam Naam. In this opening chapter, we explore the universal call to harmony and the significance of the divine melody that echoes through the ages."

In the hushed corners of existence, where the heart seeks solace and the spirit yearns for connection, there emerges a subtle call—a call that transcends the cacophony of daily life, echoing through the vast chambers of the soul. This call, gentle yet persistent, is the timeless invitation to attune oneself to the divine melody of Raam Naam, the universal vibration that beckons seekers on a journey of harmony.

The Universal Echo

The call of harmony is not bound by the constraints of time or space. It is a universal resonance that has reverberated through the ages, drawing the attention of those attuned to the subtle frequencies of the divine. This cosmic call speaks to the core of human existence, inviting individuals to step beyond the ordinary and embark on a quest for a higher, more harmonious reality.

Seeking the Source

For centuries, mystics, sages, and seekers from diverse cultural backgrounds have heeded the call of harmony. Whether through the intricate verses of the Vedas, the poetic expressions of the Bhakti movement, or the teachings of enlightened beings, the call resounds like a gentle melody, guiding hearts toward a source of sublime tranquillity—the essence of Raam Naam.

The Dissonance of Modern Life

In the hustle and bustle of modern existence, the call of harmony often becomes muffled amid the clamour of worldly pursuits. The dissonance of daily life, characterized by stress, anxiety, and the ceaseless pursuit of material success, can drown out the subtle notes of the divine melody. Yet, the call persists, awaiting the moment when the weary soul turns its attention inward, seeking a sanctuary within the harmonious realms of Raam Naam.

Awakening to the Call

To heed the call of harmony is to awaken to a higher awareness, transcending the limitations of the material world. It is an acknowledgment that there is a rhythm underlying the chaos, a melody in the mid of the noise—an eternal call that invites the seeker to dance in harmony with the cosmos.

The Promise of Inner Peace

The call of harmony promises more than mere escape from the tribulations of life; it holds the key to inner peace and spiritual fulfilment. As the seeker responds to this divine invitation, a transformative journey unfolds, leading towards the discovery of a sacred space within, where the resonance of Raam Naam awaits like a timeless melody, ready to harmonize with the symphony of existence.

Opening the Heart

Responding to the call of harmony requires an opening of the heart, a willingness to listen beyond the superficial layers of reality. It beckons individuals to shed the burdens of ego and prejudice, creating space for the divine melody to penetrate the soul and guide the way toward a more harmonious existence.

The Journey Begins

As we embark on the exploration of Raam Naam, let us attune our hearts to the call of harmony. In the chapters that follow, we will unravel the profound teachings, practices, and stories that illuminate the path towards the essence of Raam Naam—the divine melody that unites the seeker with the eternal rhythm of the cosmos. In each step of this journey, may the call of harmony resonate within, guiding us towards the timeless sanctuary where the soul and the divine dance in perfect unity.

TWO
ORIGINS IN THE VEDAS

"Trace the roots of Raam Naam to the ancient Vedic scriptures, where the cosmic vibrations were first glimpsed. Uncover the mystical connection between the divine sound and the profound teachings embedded in the Vedas."

To comprehend the essence of Raam Naam, we must journey back to the ancient corridors of wisdom, where the celestial hymns of the Vedas resound with the primordial vibrations of creation. It is within these sacred verses that the origins of Raam Naam find their roots, entwined with the profound teachings that transcend the boundaries of time and space.

The Cosmic Symphony

The Vedas, regarded as the oldest scriptures in Hinduism, are a repository of divine knowledge that encapsulates the essence of existence itself. Within these hymns, the sages perceived the cosmic symphony—the reverberation of the ultimate reality that permeates every particle of the universe. It is in this symphony that the seed of Raam Naam was planted, awaiting discovery by those with hearts attuned to the subtle nuances of the divine melody.

The Sound of Creation

Embedded within the Vedas is the understanding that the universe emanates from an eternal sound, the primal vibration known as "**OM**" This sound, symbolizing the essence of the Supreme Reality, is the resonance that sets the cosmic dance in motion. Raam Naam, too, is an echo of this cosmic sound, a manifestation of the divine vibration that underlies the entire tapestry of creation.

Raam in the Rigveda

The Rigveda, the oldest of the four Vedas, provides glimpses of the divine through hymns dedicated to various deities. Amidst these verses, we find references to the concept of Raam, not merely as a historical figure but as a symbol of the cosmic order—Dharma. The sages recognized Raam as an embodiment of righteousness, and in chanting Raam, they sought alignment with the universal harmony.

The Upanishadic Insights

As the Vedic era transitioned into the age of Upanishads, the focus shifted from ritualistic practices to the exploration of profound metaphysical truths. The Upanishads, considered the culmination of Vedic thought, delve into the nature of the ultimate reality (Brahman) and the interconnectedness of all existence. Raam Naam, in this context, becomes a vehicle for realizing the oneness with Brahman, a tool to attune the individual soul (atman) to the cosmic soul (Paramatman).

The Essence of Sacrifice

In the Vedic rituals, sacrificial ceremonies known as Yajnas were performed to invoke divine blessings. The chanting of sacred mantras, including the name of Raam, was an integral part of these ceremonies. The essence of sacrifice in the Vedic context lies not in material offerings but in the surrender of the ego, a theme mirrored in the later teachings associated with Raam Naam.

Raam Naam: A Divine Mantra

Within the Vedas, Raam Naam is not just a historical anecdote or a cultural symbol—it is a divine mantra, a key to unlock the gates of spiritual realization. The repetition of Raam's name is akin to invoking the cosmic vibrations embedded in the Vedic hymns, aligning the individual consciousness with the eternal rhythm of the universe.

Bridging Time and Space

As we explore the origins of Raam Naam in the Vedas, we find a bridge that spans the vastness of time and space. The divine melody, encapsulated in the cosmic symphony of the Vedas, echoes through the corridors of history, inviting seekers of every era to partake in the timeless journey of self-discovery and spiritual awakening.

In the subsequent chapters, we will further unravel the threads of Raam Naam, tracing its evolution through the corridors of spiritual traditions and unveiling the profound teachings that have enriched the tapestry of human understanding.

THREE
RAMA AND THE RAMAYANA

"Dive into the epic tale of Lord Rama and the Ramayana, discovering the timeless wisdom encapsulated in the narrative. Explore how the life of Rama serves as a beacon, guiding seekers towards the transformative power of Raam Naam."

In the sacred epic of the Ramayana, we encounter the timeless tale of virtue, devotion, and the divine journey of Lord Rama—a narrative that serves not only as a literary masterpiece but as a profound spiritual guide. Within the verses of the Ramayana, the essence of Raam Naam unfolds, weaving a tapestry that transcends the boundaries of time and space, inviting seekers to delve into the depths of their own souls.

The Epic Narrative

Attributed to the sage Valmiki, the Ramayana narrates the life and exploits of Lord Rama, the seventh avatar of Lord Vishnu. Set in the Treta Yuga, the epic unfolds with Rama's exile, his wife Sita's abduction by the demon king Ravana, and Rama's subsequent quest to rescue her. The narrative is interwoven with moral dilemmas, familial bonds, and the triumph of dharma (righteousness) over adharma (unrighteousness).

Rama: The Embodiment of Virtue

Lord Rama is not merely a historical figure; he is an archetype, the very embodiment of virtue and righteousness. His unwavering commitment to dharma, his humility in the face of adversity, and his compassion towards all beings make him a timeless symbol of the divine order. Chanting the name of Rama is, in essence, an invocation of these virtues, a recognition of the eternal principles embedded in the cosmic symphony.

Sita and Raam Naam

The abduction of Sita and Rama's relentless pursuit to rescue her form the crux of the Ramayana. Sita, representing the divine feminine and the pure soul, becomes a metaphor for the seeker's connection with the divine. The resonance of Raam Naam echoes through Rama's unwavering love for Sita, symbolizing the eternal bond between the individual soul and the Supreme Soul.

Hanuman's Devotion

The character of Hanuman, the devoted monkey-god, exemplifies unparalleled devotion and selfless service. His leap to bring the medicinal herb to heal Lakshmana and his fearless journey to Lanka underscore the power of unwavering faith in the divine. Hanuman's devotion to Lord Rama serves as an inspiration for seekers, emphasizing the transformative potential of Raam Naam in cultivating steadfast love and surrender to the divine.

Raam Naam in the Ramayana

The Ramayana is not merely a historical narrative; it is a spiritual guide that subtly introduces the significance of Raam Naam. In times of distress, Rama, Sita, and Hanuman utter the divine name, infusing the epic with the potency of sacred vibrations. Through the repetition of Raam Naam, the characters find solace, strength, and divine guidance, highlighting the transformative power of chanting in navigating the challenges of life.

Tulsidas and the Ramcharitmanas

The impact of the Ramayana extends beyond its literary form. Tulsidas, a saint and poet of the Bhakti movement, further popularized the narrative through his magnum opus, the

Ramcharitmanas. This Awadhi retelling not only served to make the epic accessible to the masses but also emphasized the importance of chanting Raam Naam as a direct path to spiritual realization.

The Inner Ramayana

As seekers delve into the Ramayana, they recognize that it is not merely an external narrative but a reflection of the inner journey. The battles fought, the trials faced, and the eventual triumph over the forces of ego and illusion mirror the challenges encountered on the spiritual path. Raam Naam becomes the guiding light, offering solace and strength to navigate the inner landscapes and awaken the latent divinity within.

Conclusion

In the pages of the Ramayana, the divine melody of Raam Naam unfolds, inviting seekers to embark on a spiritual odyssey. Lord Rama, with his exemplary virtues, becomes a beacon illuminating the path of righteousness and devotion. As we move forward in this exploration of Raam Naam, let us carry the lessons of the Ramayana in our hearts, recognizing that the divine melody is not confined to the epic's verses but resonates eternally, inviting us to partake in the universal harmony.

FOUR
SAINTS AND SAGES OF BHAKTI

"Meet the luminaries of the Bhakti movement, including Tulsidas, Kabir, and Surdas, who played pivotal roles in popularizing Raam Naam. Through their verses and devotion, witness the blossoming of the divine melody in the hearts of the masses."

In the tapestry of Indian spirituality, the Bhakti movement emerged as a vibrant thread, weaving the fabric of devotion, love, and a profound connection with the divine. Through the verses and teachings of saints and sages, the essence of Raam Naam found a resonant chord, transcending religious boundaries and cultural distinctions. In this chapter, we explore the lives and contributions of some luminaries of the Bhakti movement who played pivotal roles in popularizing Raam Naam.

Kabir: Weaver of Mystical Verses

Kabir, a weaver by profession and a mystic at heart, stands as an icon of the Bhakti movement. His verses, collected in the "Bijak," resonate with the simplicity of Raam Naam and the universal nature of divine love. Kabir's teachings emphasize the direct and personal experience of God, encouraging seekers to go beyond rituals and dogmas and to connect with the divine through the chanting of God's name.

Tulsidas: The Saint Poet

Tulsidas, a devotee of Lord Rama, composed the magnum opus "Ramcharitmanas," an Awadhi retelling of the Ramayana. Through his poetic genius, Tulsidas conveyed the significance of Raam Naam as a transformative force. His devotion to Lord Rama and the power of Raam Naam served as an inspiration for generations, solidifying the connection between the divine name and the path of bhakti.

Surdas: Melodious Devotion

Surdas, a blind poet-saint, enriched the Bhakti movement with his devotional compositions dedicated to Lord Krishna. His verses, often sung in melodious tunes, expressed the depth of love and surrender to the divine. While Surdas may be renowned for his Krishna bhakti, the essence of Raam Naam is ever-present in the universal themes of devotion, humility, and divine connection found in his poetry.

Mirabai: A Princess of Devotion

Mirabai, a Rajput princess, defied social norms and dedicated her life to Krishna bhakti. Her devotional songs, steeped in love and longing, echo the essence of Raam Naam in their universal appeal. Mira's unwavering devotion, expressed through her poetry and songs, serves as a testament to the transformative power of bhakti and the divine melody that unites all hearts.

Namdev: Weaver of Unity

Namdev, a saint from Maharashtra, transcended caste and creed through his devotion to Vithoba, a form of Lord Krishna. His abhangas (devotional songs) emphasized the oneness of God and the universality of divine love. Namdev's teachings highlight the inclusivity inherent in Raam Naam, breaking down societal barriers and fostering unity among devotees.

The Bhakti Synthesis

Collectively, these saints and sages of the Bhakti movement created a rich tapestry of devotional literature and music, emphasizing the simplicity and accessibility of divine connection. While their individual paths may have been diverse, the common thread of Raam Naam united them in a shared devotion to the divine. Their teachings served as a catalyst for the democratization of spirituality, offering a direct and personal connection with the divine to people from all walks of life.

The Transformative Power of Raam Naam

Through the lives and teachings of these Bhakti saints, we witness the transformative power of Raam Naam in shaping the spiritual landscape of India. The universal appeal of chanting the divine name transcended linguistic, cultural, and social boundaries, leaving an indelible mark on the collective consciousness.

Bhakti's Enduring Legacy

The legacy of the Bhakti movement endures, and the echoes of Raam Naam persist in the hymns and verses that continue to inspire spiritual seekers. As we delve into the teachings of these saints and sages, let us recognize the timeless wisdom they imparted—an invitation to experience the divine through the simplicity of devotion and the profound resonance of Raam Naam.

FIVE

THE ART OF CHANTING

"Unearth the art and science of chanting Raam Naam. This chapter delves into the practical aspects of the practice, offering insights into creating a sacred space, the power of rhythmic repetition, and the transformative impact on the mind and soul."

In the spiritual journey, the art of chanting serves as a profound and accessible gateway to the divine. Whether it be the rhythmic repetition of sacred sounds or the melodic recitation of divine names, chanting has been a universal practice across cultures and traditions. In this chapter, we explore the nuances of the art of chanting, with a particular focus on the transformative power of Raam Naam.

The Sacred Sounds

Chanting, at its essence, is an ancient practice that involves the repetition of sacred sounds or mantras. These sounds, often drawn from ancient scriptures, carry vibrational frequencies that resonate with the cosmic energy and create a harmonious connection between the individual soul and the divine. In the art of chanting, the voice becomes an instrument for invoking the sacred.

Raam Naam: A Divine Mantra

Raam Naam, the divine name of Lord Rama, is more than a sequence of syllables—it is a mantra, a potent tool for spiritual awakening. The rhythmic repetition of Raam Naam serves to quiet the mind, allowing practitioners to move beyond the noise of daily life and attune themselves to the subtle vibrations of the divine.

Creating a Sacred Space

The art of chanting often begins with the creation of a sacred space—a physical or mental environment where the practitioner can immerse themselves in the practice. This space can be as simple as a quiet room, a serene natural setting, or an inner sanctuary within the mind. The sacred space provides a conducive environment for the resonance of Raam Naam to unfold.

Rhythmic Repetition and Breath

Chanting is intrinsically linked to rhythm, and the repetition of Raam Naam often follows a rhythmic pattern. The alignment of chanting with breath creates a meditative cadence, facilitating a deep connection between body, mind, and spirit. The rhythmic repetition of the divine name becomes a vehicle for mindfulness, leading practitioners into a state of inner stillness.

Devotion and Intent

The art of chanting is not a mechanical exercise, but a heart-cantered practice infused with devotion and intent. The sincerity with which one chants Raam Naam determines the depth of the practice. Devotion transforms chanting from a mere vocalization into a communion with the divine, a conversation between the individual soul and the Supreme Soul.

Silence Between the Chants

In the art of chanting, the silence between the chants is as significant as the sound itself. These moments of stillness allow the practitioner to absorb the vibrations, reflect on the meaning of the divine name, and experience the subtle shifts in consciousness. The interplay of sound and silence becomes a dance, guiding the practitioner towards a state of inner harmony.

Integration into Daily Life

The art of chanting extends beyond formal meditation sessions—it integrates into the rhythm of daily life. Whether walking, cooking, or engaging in routine activities, practitioners can carry the resonance of Raam Naam with them. This continuous thread of chanting becomes a constant companion, infusing every moment with the divine melody.

Insights and Inner Transformation

Through the consistent practice of chanting Raam Naam, practitioners often report profound insights and inner transformations. The repetitive nature of chanting acts as a subtle purifier, clearing the mind of distractions and negativity. As the layers of the ego dissolve, individuals may experience a heightened sense of clarity, peace, and spiritual connection.

The Community of Chanters

Chanting Raam Naam is not confined to solitary practice; it often extends to communal gatherings. The collective resonance of voices chanting together creates a powerful energy that amplifies the transformative impact. The community of chanters becomes a support system, fostering a shared journey towards spiritual elevation.

Conclusion

In the art of chanting Raam Naam, we discover a timeless practice that transcends cultural, religious, and linguistic boundaries. The rhythmic repetition of the divine name is a sacred dance, a melody that resonates with the cosmic symphony. As we continue to explore the transformative power of Raam Naam, let the art of chanting be a guiding light, leading us towards the inner sanctuary where the divine melody harmonizes with the soul's yearning for unity.

SIX
HARMONY IN DIVERSITY

"Explore the inclusive nature of Raam Naam, transcending religious boundaries and embracing the diversity of spiritual paths. Witness how the divine melody harmonizes with the universal essence present in every faith and culture."

In the kaleidoscope of existence, diversity is the vibrant palette that colours the fabric of the universe. Amidst the myriad expressions of life, the concept of harmony in diversity emerges as a profound and universal truth. This chapter explores how the essence of Raam Naam embraces and celebrates the richness of diversity, transcending the boundaries that often divide humanity.

Unity in the Cosmic Symphony

Raam Naam, as a universal vibration, resonates with the understanding that diversity is an inherent aspect of the cosmic symphony. Everyone, like a unique note, contributes to the harmonious composition of the universe. The divine melody acknowledges the diversity of creation as a manifestation of the one divine source, emphasizing unity amidst multiplicity.

Raam as the Embodiment of Unity

In the Bhakti traditions, Lord Rama is often revered as the embodiment of dharma and unity. His life and teachings, as depicted in the Ramayana, transcend social, cultural, and religious boundaries. Raam Naam, in this context, becomes a unifying force, inviting individuals of diverse backgrounds to connect with the universal principles embedded in the divine name.

Bhakti Saints and Inclusivity

The saints and sages of the Bhakti movement, such as Kabir, Tulsidas, Surdas, and Mirabai, exemplified the spirit of inclusivity. Their teachings emphasized that the divine is not confined to any form, religion, or language. Raam Naam, as a focal point of devotion, transcends sectarian divisions, inviting people from all walks of life to join in the harmonious expression of love for the divine.

Chanting Across Cultures

The practice of chanting Raam Naam has transcended cultural boundaries, finding resonance in diverse spiritual traditions. Whether in the bhakti-rich landscapes of India, the serene monasteries of Tibet, or the vibrant congregations of Western spiritual seekers, the universal appeal of Raam Naam serves as a bridge, uniting hearts across diverse cultures and backgrounds.

Raam Naam in Different Traditions

The universality of Raam Naam is evident in its presence across various religious and cultural traditions. In Hinduism, it is central to the Bhakti movement; in Sikhism, Guru Nanak's hymns emphasize the oneness of God using the name Raam; in Sufi poetry, Raam is a symbol of divine love. This inclusivity underscores the ability of Raam Naam to transcend the confines of any faith.

The Melting Pot of Humanity

Harmony in diversity is not a homogenization of uniqueness but a celebration of the rich tapestry woven by the collective diversity of humanity. Raam Naam invites individuals to recognize the divine essence in themselves and others, fostering a sense of interconnectedness that goes beyond external differences.

Embracing Differences

The practice of Raam Naam encourages the embrace of differences as complementary aspects of the divine design. Just as different musical notes contribute to the beauty of a melody, diverse individuals contribute to the harmonious symphony of existence. Raam Naam becomes a mantra of acceptance, fostering a mindset that cherishes diversity as an integral aspect of the cosmic dance.

Building Bridges Through Raam Naam

In a world often marked by division and discord, Raam Naam emerges as a bridge that spans the chasms of separation. When chanted with sincerity, it dissolves the illusion of separateness and promotes a sense of unity. The collective chanting of Raam Naam in diverse gatherings becomes a powerful force that builds bridges and transcends the barriers that divide humanity.

Raam Naam as the Common Thread

As we navigate the diverse landscapes of human experience, Raam Naam serves as a common thread that weaves through the stories of countless lives. In the chapters of history, across the pages of different cultures and faiths, the resonance of Raam Naam echoes as a reminder of our shared humanity and interconnected spiritual heritage.

Conclusion

Harmony in diversity is not a utopian ideal but an inherent truth that Raam Naam unveils. It invites each seeker to recognize the divine melody within themselves and others, fostering a world where the tapestry of humanity is celebrated in all its diverse hues. As we continue our exploration of Raam Naam, let us carry the awareness of harmony in diversity, allowing the divine melody to unite us in a celebration of our shared existence.

SEVEN

The Inner Symphony

—♥—

"Journey into the depths of the inner self, where the symphony of Raam Naam resonates. Discover the transformative power of this divine melody as it cleanses the mind, awakens the spirit, and unveils the true nature of the self."

In the quiet chambers of the soul, a profound symphony unfolds—a melody that resonates with the cosmic vibrations and echoes the timeless truth of Raam Naam. This inner symphony, often unheard amidst the clamour of daily life, is a sacred composition that guides the seeker on a journey of self-discovery, spiritual awakening, and harmonious integration with the cosmic rhythms.

The Rhythms of the Soul

The inner symphony is not a mere metaphor; it is a pulsating rhythm that emanates from the depths of the soul. Just as the heart beats in cadence with life, the inner symphony is the subtle resonance of the soul's connection with the divine. Raam Naam becomes the sacred refrain that harmonizes the individual soul with the cosmic soul, creating a melody that transcends the boundaries of time and space.

Quieting the Discordant Notes

In the hustle and bustle of daily life, the mind often becomes a cacophony of discordant thoughts and emotions. The inner symphony, however, invites the seeker to quiet the dissonance and attune the mind to the subtler frequencies of Raam Naam. The rhythmic repetition of the divine name becomes a powerful tool for centering the mind and inviting a sense of inner calm.

Resonance in Contemplative Silence

The inner symphony is often most palpable in moments of contemplative silence. As the seeker turns inward, the sacred vibrations of Raam Naam resonate in the silence between thoughts, creating a space where the soul can commune with the divine. In this inner sanctuary, the symphony unfolds, inviting the seeker to listen with the heart rather than the ears.

The Dance of Mind and Breath

The inner symphony orchestrates a dance between the mind and breath. With each rhythmic repetition of Raam Naam, the breath becomes a partner in the cosmic dance, guiding the seeker into a state of mindful awareness. The synchronicity of mind and breath becomes a gateway to the inner realms, where the divine melody plays in the background of consciousness.

Unveiling the Layers of Self

As the seeker delves deeper into the practice of Raam Naam, the layers of the self-begin to unveil. The inner symphony is a journey through these layers—peeling away the veils of ego, illusion, and conditioning. With each chant, the seeker moves closer to the core of their being, where the pure resonance of the soul converges with the cosmic melody.

Moments of Profound Insight

The inner symphony often gifts the seeker with moments of profound insight. These insights may manifest as a deep understanding of the self, a clarity of purpose, or a heightened perception of the interconnectedness of all existence. Raam Naam becomes the guide, leading the seeker through the labyrinth of the inner landscape to the realms of higher consciousness.

Harmony in Relationships

The inner symphony extends beyond the individual self, influencing the dynamics of relationships. As the seeker becomes attuned to the divine melody within, the vibrations of Raam Naam radiate outward, fostering harmonious connections with others. The practice becomes a bridge that unites hearts, transcending differences and nurturing a sense of oneness.

Transformative Power of Surrender

At the heart of the inner symphony lies the transformative power of surrender. The seeker, in chanting Raam Naam, surrenders the ego and individual will to the divine flow. This surrender is not a relinquishment of personal agency but a harmonious alignment with the cosmic will, allowing the seeker to navigate the currents of life with grace and resilience.

Integration of the Inner Symphony

The practice of Raam Naam is not a compartmentalized endeavour but an integrated way of life. The inner symphony seamlessly weaves into the fabric of daily existence, influencing thoughts, actions, and interactions. The seeker becomes a living instrument through which the divine melody expresses itself, creating a life that resonates with the harmony of the cosmos.

Conclusion

As we explore the inner symphony guided by Raam Naam, let us recognize that this sacred composition is not a distant melody but an intimate part of our existence. The resonance of the divine name invites us to listen, to attune ourselves to the subtle vibrations within, and to dance to the rhythm of the cosmic symphony. In the chapters that follow, we will delve deeper into the transformative power of Raam Naam, discovering how this inner symphony leads us towards spiritual elevation and unity with the eternal rhythm of the universe.

EIGHT

THE DAILY RHYTHM

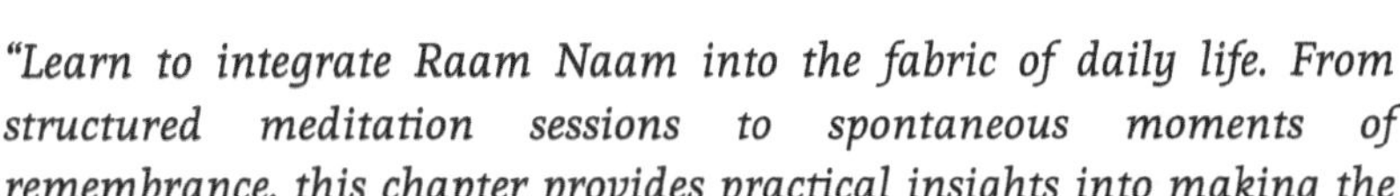

"Learn to integrate Raam Naam into the fabric of daily life. From structured meditation sessions to spontaneous moments of remembrance, this chapter provides practical insights into making the divine melody a constant companion on life's journey."

In the fabric of daily life, there exists a rhythm—a pulsating cadence that governs our waking hours, guiding the flow of activities, thoughts, and emotions. Within this rhythmic tapestry, the practice of Raam Naam emerges as a sacred thread, weaving through the moments of our day and infusing the mundane with the sublime. This chapter explores the art of integrating Raam Naam into the daily rhythm, transforming routine into a spiritual practice.

Awakening with Gratitude

The daily rhythm begins with the awakening of consciousness from the realm of sleep. Infuse this sacred moment with gratitude by starting the day with the chanting of Raam Naam. As the first rays of sunlight illuminate the world, let the divine melody set the tone for a day grounded in spiritual awareness.

Setting Intentions with Raam Naam

Before diving into the demands of the day, take a moment to set intentions. Whether through silent contemplation or a dedicated chanting session, align your goals and actions with the sacred vibrations of Raam Naam. Let this practice serve as a compass, guiding your decisions and actions with clarity and purpose.

Raam Naam in Everyday Tasks

The daily rhythm unfolds through routine tasks—preparing meals, commuting, working, and attending to responsibilities. Infuse these activities with the resonance of Raam Naam. Whether silently in the mind or softly on the lips, let the divine melody accompany you, transforming ordinary moments into opportunities for spiritual connection.

Midday Reflection and Reset

As the day progresses, take moments for midday reflection. Amidst the hustle, pause to chant Raam Naam, allowing the divine vibrations to rejuvenate and reset your inner state. This midday reset becomes a bridge between morning and afternoon, fostering a continuous awareness of the sacred within the routine.

Afternoon Renewal

The afternoon, often a period of increased activity, invites a renewal of focus and energy. Dedicate a few moments to the practice of Raam Naam, drawing upon its revitalizing power. Let the divine melody anchor you, offering a moment of serenity amidst the demands of the day.

Evening Contemplation

As the day winds down, engage in the practice of Raam Naam during evening contemplation. Reflect on the events of the day, acknowledging moments of gratitude and lessons learned. The divine melody becomes a companion in introspection, guiding you towards a state of inner calm and spiritual reflection.

Sunset Meditation

At the threshold of night, as the sun sets and darkness descends, partake in a sunset meditation with Raam Naam. Allow the celestial transition to mirror the quieting of the mind. In the soft glow of twilight, chant the divine name, inviting a sense of peace and serenity to settle within.

Nightly Surrender

Before entering the realm of dreams, engage in the practice of nightly surrender with Raam Naam. Let the divine melody accompany you into the world of sleep, serving as a guardian of the subconscious. Surrender the worries of the day, embracing the soothing vibrations of Raam Naam as a lullaby for the soul.

Cultivating Presence

The daily rhythm with Raam Naam is not about rigid structure but cultivating presence. It is an invitation to infuse every moment with mindful awareness, recognizing the divine in the ordinary. Whether in the bustling activities of the day or the quietude of the night, Raam Naam becomes the continuous thread that ties each moment to the sacred.

Creating Sacred Spaces

Integrate the practice of Raam Naam into dedicated sacred spaces within your home or workplace. These spaces serve as reminders of the divine presence, providing havens where the daily rhythm seamlessly intertwines with the eternal rhythm of the cosmos. Let these sacred spaces be adorned with the vibrations of Raam Naam, fostering an atmosphere of spiritual sanctity.

Conclusion

As we navigate the tapestry of the daily rhythm with Raam Naam, let us recognize that the sacred and the mundane need not be separate. By weaving the divine melody into the fabric of our routine, we elevate the ordinary to the extraordinary. In the chapters that follow, we delve deeper into the transformative potential of Raam Naam, exploring how this practice becomes a guiding light in the daily rhythm, leading us towards a life of spiritual fulfilment and harmonious connection with the cosmos.

NINE

RESONANCE IN ADVERSITY

—❦—

"Explore the resilience and strength that Raam Naam provides in moments of adversity. Through stories and teachings, witness how the divine melody becomes a source of solace, guiding individuals through the challenges of life."

In the crucible of life's challenges, the practice of Raam Naam becomes a steadfast companion, offering solace, strength, and a reservoir of resilience. This chapter explores the profound resonance of Raam Naam in the face of adversity, illuminating how the divine melody becomes a source of inner fortitude, guiding the seeker through the storms of life.

The Echo of Raam Naam in Turbulent Times

Adversity, in its various forms, is an inevitable aspect of the human experience. In times of turbulence and uncertainty, Raam Naam emerges as a timeless anchor, resonating within the heart of the seeker. The divine melody becomes a refuge, echoing through the corridors of the soul, providing solace and clarity amid life's storms.

Chanting Through the Storm

Adversity often gives rise to a whirlwind of emotions and thoughts. Amid this turbulence, the rhythmic repetition of Raam Naam serves as a steady chant, grounding the mind and allowing the seeker to navigate the challenges with a heart. The divine resonance becomes a compass, guiding through the darkness towards the light within.

Raam Naam as a Shield

In the face of adversity, Raam Naam acts as a shield, protecting the seeker from the arrows of despair and doubt. The vibrational frequencies of the divine name create an energetic barrier, allowing the practitioner to face challenges with resilience and courage. The practice becomes a sanctuary within, where the storms may rage, but the inner serenity remains unshaken.

Transforming Suffering into Compassion

Raam Naam transforms adversity into a crucible for spiritual alchemy. The resonance of the divine melody transmutes suffering into compassion. As the seeker chants in the face of personal trials, empathy deepens, and the heart expands to encompass the collective human experience. Adversity becomes a shared journey, and Raam Naam becomes a bridge connecting all hearts in the symphony of compassion.

Surrendering in the Midst of Challenges

Adversity often invites the seeker to surrender—the act of relinquishing control and trusting in the divine plan. Raam Naam becomes the mantra of surrender, a soothing balm for the wounded heart. In the midst of challenges, the practitioner chants with the understanding that, just as the divine melody orchestrates the cosmos, it also weaves through the intricate patterns of personal destiny.

Illuminating the Path of Faith

In moments of adversity, faith is a guiding light that pierces through the darkness. Raam Naam becomes the embodiment of faith, a luminous presence that illuminates the path even when the way forward seems obscured. The practice nurtures an unwavering trust in the divine order, fostering a resilience rooted in the recognition that every challenge carries within it the seed of growth.

The Healing Power of Raam Naam

Adversity often leaves wounds—both seen and unseen. Raam Naam serves as a healing balm, soothing the wounds of the heart and mind. The resonance of the divine melody penetrates the depths of the soul, bringing comfort, restoration, and a profound sense of inner peace. In the practice, the seeker discovers that Raam Naam is not just a sound but a healing vibration that transcends the limitations of suffering.

Embracing Impermanence

In the face of adversity, Raam Naam becomes a reminder of the impermanence of all things. The divine melody invites the seeker to embrace the transient nature of challenges, recognizing that just as the notes of a melody rise and fall, so too do the tides of life. This understanding brings a sense of equanimity, allowing the practitioner to navigate adversity with grace and acceptance.

Resonating Compassion in the World

As the seeker encounters adversity, Raam Naam becomes a catalyst for resonating compassion in the world. The practice extends beyond personal challenges, inspiring acts of kindness, empathy, and service towards others facing their own trials. The divine resonance becomes a force that ripples through the collective consciousness, fostering a world where compassion becomes the antidote to adversity.

Conclusion

In the symphony of life, adversity plays its part as a challenging movement, testing the strength and resilience of the seeker. Through the resonance of Raam Naam, the seeker discovers that even in the dissonance of adversity, there is a harmonious undertone—the eternal melody that guides, heals, and transforms. As we continue to explore the transformative power of Raam Naam, let the understanding of its resonance in adversity be a source of inspiration and courage on the spiritual journey.

TEN

UNITY IN THE DIVINE MELODY

"In the final chapter, experience the culmination of the Raam Naam journey—a unity with the divine through the sacred melody. Discover how the essence of Raam Naam transcends the individual self, weaving a tapestry of oneness that harmonizes with the cosmic symphony."

In the realm of spiritual exploration, the practice of Raam Naam unfolds as a journey towards unity—a harmonious blending of the individual soul with the cosmic soul. This chapter delves into the profound concept of unity within the divine melody, exploring how Raam Naam serves as a bridge that dissolves the illusion of separation and awakens the seeker to the oneness of existence.

The Essence of Oneness

At the heart of the divine melody is the recognition that all creation emanates from the same source—the One, the Supreme Reality, known by myriad names. Raam Naam encapsulates this understanding of oneness, inviting the seeker to chant the divine name with the awareness that it transcends the limitations of language, culture, and form.

Beyond Religious Boundaries

Raam Naam serves as a universal mantra, transcending religious boundaries and sectarian divisions. In the resonance of the divine melody, distinctions between faiths dissolve, and the seeker is drawn into the inclusive embrace of a spiritual journey that transcends dogmas. The unity found in Raam Naam becomes a testament to the universality of the divine message.

Oneness with the Cosmic Symphony

As the practitioner engages in the rhythmic repetition of Raam Naam, the individual soul becomes attuned to the cosmic symphony. The divine melody becomes the thread that weaves through the tapestry of existence, connecting every soul to the eternal source. In this unity with the cosmic symphony, the seeker recognizes the interconnectedness of all life.

Dissolving Egoic Boundaries

The ego, with its divisive tendencies, often creates a sense of separation. Raam Naam becomes the antidote to egoic boundaries, inviting the practitioner to dissolve the illusion of a separate self. In the practice, the egoic mind gradually yields to the awareness of a shared divine essence, fostering a sense of unity with all beings.

Resonance Beyond Dualities

The divine melody of Raam Naam resonates beyond the dualities of good and bad, right and wrong. It is a unifying force that transcends polarities, guiding the seeker towards a state of equanimity and acceptance. In the unity found within the divine melody, judgment and discrimination give way to an understanding that all aspects of creation contribute to the symphony of existence.

Unity in Diversity

Raam Naam celebrates the diversity of creation while emphasizing the unity that underlies this diversity. Each soul, like a unique note in a melody, contributes to the richness of the cosmic composition. In chanting Raam Naam, the seeker recognizes the beauty of diversity, understanding that unity is not the absence of differences but the harmonious coexistence of all expressions of life.

The Role of Love in Unity

Love, as a binding force, is inherent in the practice of Raam Naam. The divine melody is steeped in the essence of love—the love between the individual soul and the Supreme Soul. In the unity found within this love, the seeker experiences a profound connection with all of creation, fostering a sense of unity that extends beyond the confines of personal identity.

Unity in Service and Compassion

Raam Naam inspires acts of service and compassion, reinforcing the idea that the practice is not merely an individual endeavour but a collective journey towards unity. In selfless service, the practitioner recognizes the divine presence in others, fostering a sense of unity that transcends personal gain and reflects the interconnectedness of all souls.

Unity in Stillness

In the silent moments between chants, the seeker encounters the profound unity found in stillness. Raam Naam becomes a gateway to inner peace—a space where the boundaries of the self dissolve, and the practitioner merges with the expansive silence that underlies the divine melody. In this unity with stillness, the seeker discovers a source of profound serenity.

Conclusion

As we conclude our exploration of unity in the divine melody of Raam Naam, let us carry the awareness of oneness into our lives. The practice becomes a living testament to the unity that transcends appearances, divisions, and limitations. In the unity found within the divine melody, the seeker discovers a timeless truth—that the essence of all existence is one, and the journey towards realizing this oneness is the sacred path illuminated by Raam Naam.

www.ingramcontent.com/pod-product-compliance
Lightning Source LLC
Chambersburg PA
CBHW022123150726
47990CB00003B/1480